STRANGER
FROM SOMEWHERE IN
TIME

Crabtree Publishing Company
www.crabtreebooks.com

PMB 16A, 350 Fifth Avenue
Suite 3308
New York, NY 10118

612 Welland Avenue
St. Catharines, Ontario
Canada, L2M 5V6

McBratney, Sam.
    Stranger from Somewhere in Time / Sam McBratney ; illustrated by
Martin and Ann Chatterton.
        p. cm. -- (Yellow bananas)
    Summary: Helen and her friends assemble a time capsule, hoping that someone
from the future will find it and send it back, but things turn out differently than
anyone expected.
    ISBN 0-7787-0937-X (RHC) -- ISBN 0-7787-0983-3 (pbk.)
    [1. Time capsules--Fiction. 2. Tricks--Fiction. 3. Friendship--Fiction.] I.
Chatterton, Martin, ill. II. Chatterton, Ann,
ill. III. Title. IV. Series.
PZ7.M1218 St 2003
    [Fic]--dc21
                            2002009632
                                LC

Published by Crabtree Publishing in 2002
Published in 2000 by Egmont Children's Books Limited
Text copyright © Sam McBratney 1994
Illustrations copyright © Martin and Ann Chatterton 2000
The Author and Illustrator have asserted their moral rights.
Reinforced Hardcover Binding ISBN 0-7787-0937-X Paperback ISBN 0-7787-0983-3

1 2 3 4 5 6 7 8 9 0 Printed in Italy 0 9 8 7 6 5 4 3 2

Sam McBratney
STRANGER FROM SOMEWHERE IN TIME

Illustrated by Martin and Ann Chatterton

 YELLOW BANANAS

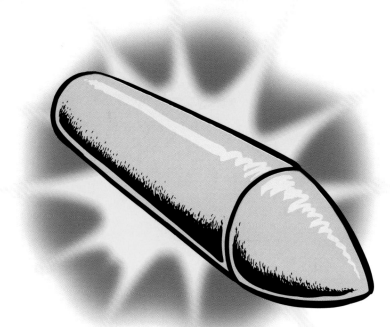

Chapter One

HAVE YOU EVER made a time capsule?

Well if you haven't, don't bother, because it will probably only get you into trouble. We wouldn't have made one either if Mrs. Fairley hadn't put the idea into our heads. She's our teacher.

"Suppose you were to send a time capsule into space?" she said. "Or bury it in the ground for ten thousand years? What would you put in it? What would you like people to find in the far distant future? There's something for you to think about over the weekend."

I nearly went to sleep there and then. Do you
want to think over the weekend? I don't. I want
to have a good time. And yet, on the way home
from school, the five of us talked about nothing
else but the time capsule.

My name is Helen.

Lorna is my friend. Her mom is a teacher and her dad was in the army in Hong Kong, so she can count up to ten in Chinese.

Then there's Bopper, who can hardly count up to ten in English. His schoolbag is like a hospital for injured books and pens.

Murdo, the youngest, is round and gentle; he was upset for days when Mrs. Fairley told him to sing quietly.

Finally there's Alan Ward, the best reader in our class. Everybody calls him Foxy. His head is full of things like time travel and computer games. You can be sure that he saves Planet Earth at least once a night from baddies like the Mad Wizard of the Universe.

"Ten thousand years," said Foxy as we passed our brand new shopping mall. "That's a long time, you know. Maybe the Daleks will have wiped us out by then."

"Exterminate, exterminate!" screamed Bopper, pointing his Dalek feelers at two ladies coming out of the shopping mall. They gave him a dirty look and walked on, unexterminated.

"Let's meet in Murdo's garage after supper," said Foxy. "We'll make our own time capsule. If everybody brings along something to bury, we can send a message into the future."

I looked at Lorna to see if she thought this was a good idea. She did.

"Listen, Foxy," I said, "there's nothing in my house that I can bury for ten thousand years."

He smiled patiently, as if my poor brain didn't understand how these things worked.

"We only have to bury the capsule for one night," he said. "We'll dig it up again in the morning. Look, I'll explain after supper, okay?"

They should have taken my advice, of course, but they didn't. It was four-to-one against me. And I didn't have a clue what to bring along for the Great Burying Ceremony!

Chapter Two

I ARRIVED IN Murdo's garage with a jar of anti-wrinkle cream borrowed from my mom, a can of de-icer borrowed from Dad, and a slinky toy that used to be able to go down the stairs on its own.

Lorna had brought along sunglasses, a Mickey Mouse toothbrush, an electric plug, and an X-ray of the bone she broke last year. And a red Frisbee.

Foxy Ward had a can opener, a pocket
calculator, a package of flower seeds, a
magnifying glass, and a whistle. Since this whole
crazy idea came from him he also supplied the
time capsule – a white plastic box.

"My turn!" announced Bopper, laying a

chewed-up old shoe on the garage bench,
and then a piece of brown bread. Next came
a disposable diaper, $400 of Monopoly money,
and a dead daddy longlegs. Nobody said a word
as Foxy placed all of it into the time capsule. We
were all speechless.

Now it was Murdo's turn. He only managed to
think of two things. One was an oven mitt
and the other was a package wrapped in bright
blue paper.

"That's my birthday
present," he said. "It
was in the cupboard
under the sink. Mom
doesn't know I
found it. I'm not
supposed to have
it until next week."

"What's in it?"
asked Bopper.

"Dunno, I
haven't opened it."

Everyone loves the
mystery present. I could feel three soft lumps
when I took it into my hands. Foxy shook it
and Bopper sniffed at it, but Murdo's present
didn't rattle or smell.

"Careful! I don't want anything to happen to
it," he said.

"It won't," Foxy assured him. "Now, everybody put your names on this computer print-out and we'll seal the whole thing up."

The print-out said:

Dear Stranger from Somewhere in Time,
These things were buried here by people
at the beginning of the twenty-first
century. If you have time travel, come
back and visit us. We all live in
Mountview Avenue, except Bopper.

Signed: Foxy Ward
Helen Waller
Bopper Travolta Winston
Lorna Lee Murdoch

We all signed with our full names. The white
time capsule was taped up with our things and
the note inside; then we carried it behind
Murdo's house and buried it.

"Okay," Foxy said. "We'll come back tomorrow morning at nine thirty and see if he wants to contact us."

"Who?" asked Lorna.

"The Stranger from Somewhere in Time."

"He might be a she," I pointed out. "And how will this Stranger from Somewhere in Time get

in touch with us? Can I remind everyone that I'm only leaving my mom's anti-wrinkle cream here for one night, not ten thousand years!"

"Look," said Foxy, "after ten thousand years they find the capsule, but they come back to our present. We won't know that any time has passed. Understand?"

Of course I didn't understand, but I wasn't going to admit it.

In bed that night I thought that maybe Foxy's words made a weird sort of sense. Perhaps in years to come people would discover how to travel in time. After all, people from the Stone Age would freak out if they saw what we can do nowadays. I tried to zoom my mind forward to the year 12000. What would they think of anti-wrinkle cream and an oven mitt? Not to mention a mystery blue present and a disposable diaper!

Chapter Three

THE NEXT MORNING it was wet and muddy. It had poured rain all night long. I met Lorna in her new jacket and bright yellow rubber boots. She was carrying her fancy new camera with all its extra gizmos.

"If it comes I'll ask it to say cheese," she giggled.

We met Bopper at the corner of Mountview. When the three of us reached Murdo's house, he came to the door looking really miserable.

20

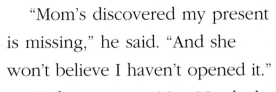

"Mom's discovered my present is missing," he said. "And she won't believe I haven't opened it."

At that moment Mrs. Murdoch appeared and she didn't look happy at all.

"Helen!" she shouted, "Have you seen a blue package? Murdo says it's buried somewhere. Who would want to bury a birthday present? The thing will be ruined for goodness sake!"

"It's in a time capsule," Bopper piped up.

"It's in a what?"

"A time capsule. We've got everything. Bread, a can opener, Frisbee, oven mitt . . ."

"And my oven mitt? You buried that, too!"

"We'll get it for you now, Mrs. Murdoch," I said quickly. "Everything is nicely wrapped up in a plastic box."

That seemed to do the trick. While his mom stood there wondering, Murdo snuck past with his coat on. Off we went, picking up a shovel from Murdo's garage on the way.

Foxy Ward was already there, standing under an arch of trees at the gloomy edge of the forest. We formed a circle as Murdo slowly began to dig.

"Get a move on, Murdo," said Bopper. "I want to see if they got the message."

"I'm not putting a shovel through my birthday present, so you'll have to wait," Murdo snapped.

But the white box did not appear. As the hole in the ground grew wide and deep, I knew it had disappeared. Along with my mother's anti-wrinkle cream. And the mystery present. And Bopper's shoe. A crazy thought went through my mind. They'll think people of our time only have one leg!

In a hurry now, Murdo scooped out more dirt – and in the middle of his shovel was a small metal box.

I wouldn't have dared to touch it, but Bopper, who doesn't have nerves, snatched it up and tore off the lid. Inside was a small, flat object.

"They've returned our message!" whispered Foxy.

We were looking at a tape cassette.

Chapter Four

WHAT WE NEEDED now was a tape recorder. Foxy said he had one in his kitchen, so naturally there was a mad dash for his house.

His mom and dad were washing the car in the driveway. They looked up as we raced by.

"Where are you going?" asked Mrs. Ward.

"Kitchen. Gotta use the tape recorder, Mom."

"Message from the future!" Bopper added breathlessly.

In went the cassette. Clunk, click, press. The little wheels began to turn and all you could hear was heavy breathing. Ours.

Then: "Yigs vur piggling tardly over vims dee plaaks."

"French!" howled Bopper.

"Shh!" said Foxy.

"Earthlings of long ago – we greet you. This is Morlag Kim, Great Lord of Time and the Many Worlds. Your gifts have pleased me."

Jeepers! I looked at Lorna and she was sucking a strand of hair. Foxy was chewing his nails.

"Where's my birthday present?" Murdo suddenly shouted.

"Shh!" Foxy hissed again.

"I, Morlag Kim, have created a time gate for you near the place where you left your gifts. Be there at three o'clock and I will show you ... the *future*."

The message ended. I examined the cassette suspiciously. If this was sent from the future, why were they using a cassette made in Japan?

"Easy," said Foxy. "They have to send us something we can use in our own time. If we were sending a message back to the olden days we wouldn't send this cassette. They wouldn't know what it was. We'd send a letter written on stone."

"Where's my present?" Murdo said again.

"Gone," said Bopper. "It's in the future with my shoe. Your mom will understand, Murdo, don't worry."

Just then Mr. Ward came in, and we decided it was time to go. He gave us a friendly wink, and that was when the truth hit me like a hammer.

He knew what was going on! Foxy's dad was
Morlag Kim.

"Of course he is, Lorna," I said to her at the
gate. "I bet Foxy put him up to it."

"Bopper thinks Morlag Kim is real," said
Lorna. "So does Murdo."

"Lorna. Bopper thinks Donald Duck is real
and poor Murdo can't think of anything but
his birthday present. That Foxy is planning
something for this afternoon, you'll see."

Chapter Five

WHEN WE MET in the field at ten to three Bopper was there, Murdo was there, I was there, and Foxy was there.

"Where's Lorna?" Bopper asked me.

"She had to go shopping."

"She's going to miss this," said Foxy. "When you go through a Time Gate you step into a different world. Another time."

He made it sound natural, like stepping into your bathroom.

"And what happens if this Morlag Kim turns

out to be a real bad dude?" I said. "He might be a monster from the future and he knows who we are and where we live, thanks to you, Alan Ward."

That was the very moment when the lights started flashing at the edge of the forest - red, yellow, blue, green. They formed a kind of colored arch over the oak trees. Step through me, they seemed to say, and find yourself in another time. Just like Star Trek.

"It's the Time Gate!" whispered Bopper. And at that moment a creature came out of the bushes.

It walked like an ape, rolling from one foot to the other in the shadows of the trees. Apes don't have square heads, though, or silver bodies. Was Morlag Kim some kind of metal beast?

"Hey, mister," yelled Bopper, "are you from the future?" Then he added, "What's it like?"

I couldn't believe what happened next. Murdo ran towards the monster yelling:

"Give me back my birthday present!"

Our Murdo, who wouldn't hurt a fly, was taking on Morlag Kim, Great Lord of Time and the Many Worlds. Alone! All for a blue package. And he didn't even know what was in it! Suddenly he picked up a stick and flung it toward the shape in the shadows.

Off came the square head (a cardboard box, sprayed silver), and Lorna yelled, "Cut that out, Murdo! Are you trying to flatten me?"

The fun was almost over now. There was no Stranger from Somewhere in Time – only Lorna in a cardboard suit. There was no Time Gate – only Foxy's flashing lights. His dad had helped him wire the circuit to a battery. Last night, he snuck back, dug up the white box, and replaced it with the cassette.

"I fooled you for a while," Foxy said.

"You did, you did," Bopper agreed.

"For about ten seconds!" I said. "Now give me back my mom's anti-wrinkle cream."

"And my X-ray," said Lorna. "That's got great sentimental value."

Foxy hid the white box in the hollow of an old tree. But the lid came loose during the night. Water had run down the inside of the tree trunk, filling up the box so that our things were soaked.

What an awful mess! The paper had come off Murdo's present, and three colored balls could now be seen between a floating diaper and a lump of soaked bread. When Foxy lifted one up, water dribbled out of it like a sponge.

"It was juggling balls!" said Bopper. Murdo's eyes filled up with great big wobbly tears. He bent down, picked up the soggy juggling balls and walked away without saying a word.

"Look, we'll have to buy him some new ones," said Lorna. "Juggling balls can't cost that much."

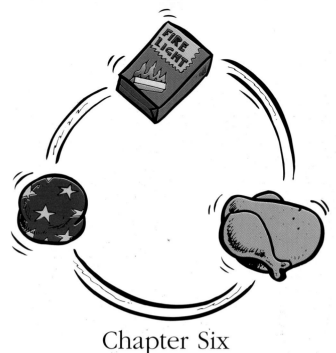

Chapter Six

HOW MUCH DID juggling balls cost?

We didn't have a clue. On the way to the shopping mall I figured they were probably more expensive than a pack of matches but cheaper than a whole cooked chicken.

Bopper, Lorna, Foxy, and I managed to scrape up ten dollars, but when we got to the store and saw the price of juggling balls, we were shocked. They were over twenty dollars for a set of three.

"We could just buy one," said Bopper.

"Don't be stupid!" snapped Lorna. "Anybody can juggle with one ball. You need three."

We came out of the store and sat down by a pool with a fountain. Our new shopping mall is that sort of place – very fancy. There are even indoor palm trees.

Lorna stared gloomily into the pool. Sparkling coins lay on the bottom, as if a pile of loose change had spilled from a giant's pocket.

"Why do people throw money into a pool?" she said.

"For good luck," I guessed.

Bopper peered in, fascinated. "Whose money is that?"

There was no sign up to warn people away.

"Nobody owns it," said Bopper. "That money might belong to anybody, you know."

It doesn't belong to you, I was about to say, but it was too late. How anyone could whip off their socks and shoes that quickly is beyond me, but suddenly Bopper's white feet were

flashing through the water like fish.

"Here's twenty-five cents!" he cried, holding up a quarter. And then another. "Look! There's more. We could buy juggling balls for everybody with the money in here!"

As the money mounted up in Bopper's hand, I started to panic.

"Get out of there, Bopper!" yelled Lorna.

When the man in the uniform appeared, I knew I should run. I couldn't. But Bopper did. He left behind a trail of wet footprints leading to the exit.

"You come back here!" yelled the security guard. Turning to us, he grabbed Foxy by the arm. "Stealing money, were you?"

"We weren't," said Foxy, white-faced.

I didn't know what to say as I stared up at the important shiny peak on the man's cap. If Morlag Kim had whisked us through his Time Gate at that moment I'd have hugged him.

"Stealing in broad daylight!"

"We weren't stealing," I said. "We were trying to stop him, weren't we, Alan?"
Foxy nodded twice, as if testing his neck.

"That boy who ran away doesn't understand about shopping malls," I added.

"He's stupid!" wailed Lorna.

Wailing was a good idea. The security guard let go of Foxy's arm and stepped back. He must have seen in our eyes that we were completely innocent.

"Well don't let me see you near that pool ever again."

Our three heads shook as we mumbled, "Never."

Foxy picked up Bopper's shoes and socks, then we rushed outside to freedom.

Chapter Seven

ABOUT HALFWAY between our shopping mall and Mountview Avenue there is an advertising board where people stick up posters to make you buy things. As we passed this board, it spoke to us.

"Psst! Are you being followed?"

Standing behind it was Bopper, in bare feet. As he put on his socks and shoes, Lorna talked to him loudly and some of the things she said weren't very nice.

But he didn't listen. He never listens.

"Do you think they'll take my toe prints?" he said. Foxy fell to the ground laughing at the idea of people taking toeprints instead of fingerprints.

"You'll have to give those coins back, Bopper," I said. "And what are you laughing at, Foxy? This is all your fault. If it wasn't for you and time travel and strangers from the future we wouldn't have ruined poor Murdo's present and nearly got arrested. Now we have to go and say sorry to him and his mom."

Murdo came to the door. Oddly enough, he was smiling.

"We're really sorry about your present, Murdo," I said.

"It's OK. Mom and I dried them with the hair dryer!"

After all that! They blow-dried everything with the hair dryer!

Murdo's mom appeared and stared at Bopper's soaking wet pants. We told her all about the money in the fountain.

"I thought it was anybody's money," said Bopper. "Now I don't know what to do."

"I'm going shopping soon," Mrs. Murdoch said. "Do you want me to take the money back for you?"

Bopper seemed relieved to empty his pockets and hand over the coins. I guess he didn't feel like a crook on the run any more.

Then we headed home. Personally I was ready to watch a nice, quiet TV show.

If we ever make a time capsule again I'm putting Alan Ward's brain into it. That'll give them plenty to think about in the far distant future.

 # YELLOW BANANAS

**Don't forget there's a whole
bunch of Yellow Bananas
to choose from:**